this Book belongs to:

_____

_____

_____

This book is dedicated to our children:
Becca, Julie, Kathy, Steve, Rob and Mike who light up our days! S.P. & R.T.

Special thanks to: Sandy Erlarger, Susie Green,
Janie Reinart and Mark Coming

A company where children have a voice.
www.maxandannie.com

Text copyright © 2002 Sandra Philipson
Illustration copyright © 2002 Robert Takatch
Max's Campfire Song copyright © 2002 Janie Reinart

Chagrin River Publishing Company
P.O. Box 173
Chagrin Falls, Ohio 44022
(440) 893-9250

First Edition
Printed in the United States of America
10 9 8 7 6 5 4 3 2 1

Library of Congress Control Number 2002093185
Philipson, Sandra.
Max and Annie's Mysterious Campfire / by Sandra Philipson; illustrated by Robert Takatch
Summary: Max and Annie explore the desert and learn how to deal peacefully
with a bully.
ISBN 1-929821-04-2 (hardcover)
[1. Adventure story—Juvenile Fiction. 2. Picture book—Juvenile Fiction.
3. English Springer Spaniels—Juvenile Fiction. 4. Friendship—Juvenile Fiction.
5. Dog story for Children. 6. Art book for children—Juvenile Fiction.]

Max and Annie's Mysterious Campfire

Table of Contents

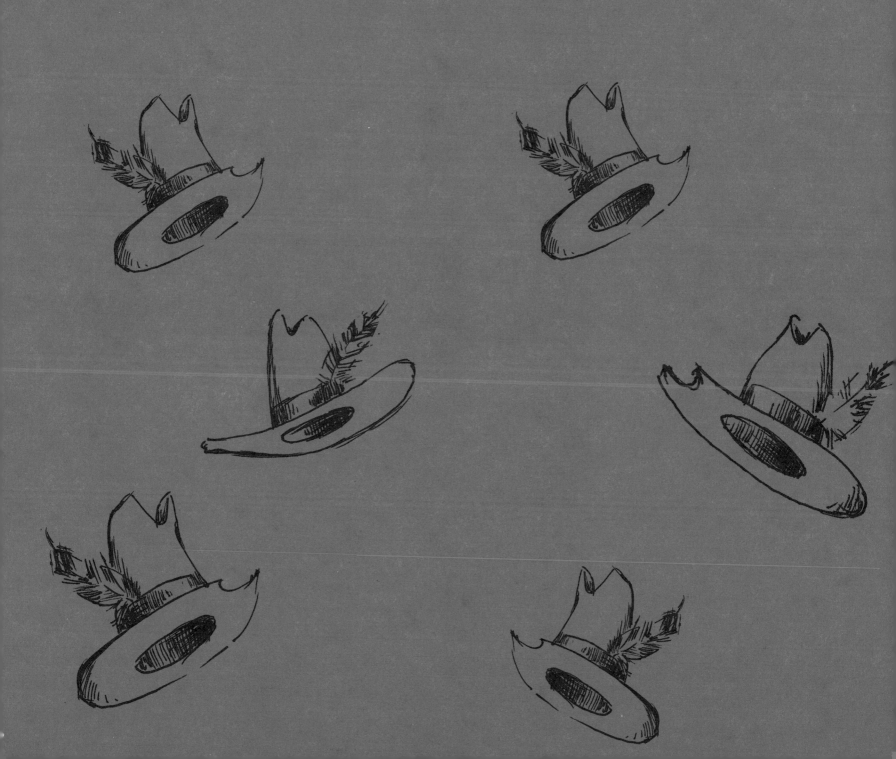

Chapter I

Escape

The Escape

Max, the English Springer Spaniel, was as mad as a wet cat. He and his sister Springer, Annie, were in a traveling dog crate surrounded by boxes and suitcases in the cargo hold of an airplane. This was Max's first plane ride, and it was not what he had imagined before the trip.

He thought that he and Annie were going to be in nice, comfy seats, eating snacks, being petted and watching a movie. Instead, he was in this dark, damp and dumpy place without snacks or a movie. Max was **insulted.** As he fumed, he decided that he would have a great adventure once they reached Arizona.

In the meantime, he cuddled up to Annie, closed his big brown eyes for a nap and dreamed of running wild out west. When he awoke, both he and Annie had landed in Tucson, Arizona, but it took a while for the dogs to be unloaded with the luggage. Max was impatient; he could hardly wait to escape and explore every new sight and smell.

Finally, Max and Annie were surrounded
by admiring cousins, aunts and uncles.
Each dog was given a cowboy hat and kerchief and loaded into the van
for the trip to Sabino Canyon where the family had planned a welcoming picnic. During
the ride all Max could think about was his escape and the adventures he might have
in this strange, new place.

While they were riding, Annie looked out the window and noticed that everything here looked so different from the woods and river that she and Max played in back home in Ohio. She nudged the sulking Max to encourage him to look out the window too.

This place **was not green.** There were no maple trees, green grass or even poison ivy. Everything looked **brown, prickly, dusty** and **dead.**

Max thought, "Where are we? This place looks like a desert **. . . Holy horse poop,** I think it is a **desert!** I can't wait to get out there and look around, and I am not doing it at the end of a leash!"

The family was anxious to show their Ohio relatives Sabino Canyon, so when the van stopped, they opened the doors quickly. This was just the opportunity Max had been waiting for. He wiggled past Mom and Annie, jumped to the ground, and **took off** running at top speed, leaving Mom holding his empty red leash.

Everyone yelled for him
to come back, but Max never turned around.
In a cloud of dust, he had started his **adventure** in the desert!

6

Chapter 2

Dogs

Desert "Dogs"

Although Annie was not surprised by Max's escape, she quickly realized that he was apt to get into a lot of trouble, off on his own like this.

"**That rascal, Max!**" exclaimed Annie. "I'd better go after him. With any luck, I can get him back here by bedtime." Annie jumped out of the van and took off in the direction of Max's dusty trail.

"**Not you, too!**" cried Mom, as she watched Annie run away.

Annie did not run quite as fast as Max since she lost her front leg to cancer a few years ago. Still, she could run faster than Mom, and she had lots of **spunk, spirit** and **smarts.** Max needed her even if he didn't realize it yet. Back home Annie was always rescuing Max from the predicaments he got himself into.

Meanwhile, Max was streaking along the canyon floor loving his freedom. His brown furry ears were **flying** in the desert breeze, and he felt lighter than air. The wide open desert stretched endlessly before him.

The sky was a brilliant blue and the sun was a hot yellow. All around them, both Max and Annie saw **big desert plants** that were nothing like the plants and trees in the woods in Ohio. Some plants were very tall and covered with spines. Some had arms and looked like giant policemen directing desert traffic. Some were small, round, spine-covered   barrels topped with yellow flower helmets.

When Max stopped to look at these strange plants, Annie caught up with him. Before she could start scolding him, a sharp **whistle** sounded a few feet away. They looked up quickly just as a small creature **popped out** of a hole in the ground.

It was a tiny **prairie dog** who gave another loud whistle and spoke very quickly in a high squeaky voice, "**Welcome strangers.** How do ya' like our desert?" Without giving Max and Annie a chance to reply, the prairie dog rattled on, "Say, we're havin' our summer **campfire** at Slippery Rock around sunset tonight. Why don't ya'll come? Just say Whoopee Pie invited you. Everyone knows me. **Gotta go.** See ya'll later."

Before Max and Annie could say anything, Whoopee disappeared down a hole to his home beneath the desert floor.

As Max and Annie stood there looking a bit bewildered, a big red bird swooped down, **squawking** and **yelling** at the dogs. **"Dang it,** you two! You scared away that prairie dog. I had my heart set on that one for lunch! Now I'll have to cruise around all afternoon looking for another. Still, I swear I'll get one of those varmints before the big campfire tonight," boasted the red-tailed hawk.

Glancing at Max, the big bird laughed and said, "I wish you were just a bit smaller. You look like a **tasty guy."**

The hawk flew away before Max or Annie could think of anything smart to say back to him or ask him where they could find Slippery Rock.

"This desert is a very **weird place;** it looks quiet, almost dead, but it sure is full of life—hungry life! Let's go," Max said to Annie.

Both dogs started to run toward a pile of rocks and plants. As usual, Max was speeding along not watching where he was going, when he tripped over two large rocks.

Immediately, he heard a grouchy voice yell, "**Ouch,** watch where you are going buddy. **You're squashing my tail!**"

Max caught himself, stopped short,
and looked around to see where the voice was
coming from. The rock was talking to him!

"Get off my tail, please, or I'll be forced to bite you," said a gravelly voice.

Max moved his paw off the rock and to his **amazement,** the rock started
to move. When he looked closer, Max realized that it was not the rock that was moving
and talking, but an animal wedged between two rocks.

Suddenly, a big **chuckwalla lizard** poked his head out from between the rocks and said, **"Whew,** that was a close call. If the red-tailed hawk had seen me, he would have had me for lunch instead of Whoopee. The name is Chuck, what's yours?"

"My name is Max, and this is my sister, Annie. That hawk sure was hungry; he wanted to eat me!" Max exclaimed. "But say, I have to know how you turned yourself into a rock. That is such a **cool trick!** I want to do that too. It could come in handy for me back home."

The chuckwalla lizard laughed and replied, "I didn't turn myself into a rock, silly dog! When I need to hide, I wedge myself between two rocks, take a deep breath, and **swell up** to fill the crack. Then nobody can pull me out, and I'm safe from those fellas who would like to eat me. You two are too big to be eaten by anyone but the mountain lion. I hear he is visiting relatives in the upper canyon today, so you should be safe until the campfire tonight."

Chapter 3

The Road
to the Campfire

"Where is Slippery Rock?" Annie asked the friendly lizard.

Chuck pointed his tail to the left and said, "See that **big *saguaro** over there? Follow the path in the direction his arm is pointing until you get to the wash or river. There's water in the wash this time of year, and Slippery Rock is right on the river bank. By the way, that tall saguaro has been pointing the way to the wash for over twenty-five years. He didn't even get his big arm until he had his 75th birthday, and now he is over **100 years old.** My great grandfather remembered that party! What a time they had! Anyway, don't miss the campfire tonight. I'll see you there."

Before Max and Annie could ask Chuck any more questions, he scooted under some brush and was gone. The campfire was still a **mystery,** and this made the dogs even more determined to attend.

*pronounced sue•wa•row

Max and Annie sniffed the air
and headed in the direction the big cactus was pointing. They thought they smelled water,
and they were feeling very **thirsty.** As they ran down the trail, a ball of dust
whizzed by them and came to a screeching halt in front of both dogs.

Until that moment, Max was convinced that he was the fastest creature in the world, or at least in Ohio, but whatever this was, it was much faster. As the dust cleared, Max saw a medium-sized bird with a very long tail. It looked familiar from Saturday morning cartoons. It was a roadrunner!

"**Wow!**" exclaimed Max. "Are you really a roadrunner? Where is your friend the coyote?"

"Who?" asked the roadrunner looking puzzled. "I don't have time to make friends with coyotes. I'm running around in search of a collard lizard, maybe a couple of small snakes, or even a kangaroo rat for my lunch. See any around?"

"Is that all you guys do here—think about **filling** your **stomachs?**" demanded Max.

The roadrunner replied, "We all want to get filled up before the big campfire tonight. No animal is allowed to come there hungry. Are you two planning on coming?"

Without waiting for an answer, the roadrunner took off, running at least **fifteen** miles an hour. Max and Annie watched in awe. Now both dogs were more intrigued than before. So they started off again, hoping to find their way to this curious campfire.

When they reached the wash, Max and Annie were surprised to see a quickly flowing river, not as big as the Chagrin River back home, but still bigger than they expected to find in the desert. As both dogs bent down to take a drink, they saw the **reflections** of other animals coming to the water. Annie looked to her left and saw a raccoon family washing their food in the river. Annie was happy to see an animal she recognized. She and Max saw **raccoons** all the time at home.

"Hi, we are Max and Annie from Ohio. Are you guys from Ohio too?" Annie asked.

The raccoon replied, "No, we were born here in Sabino Canyon. We always hang out by the water so we can rinse off our food. We have lots to wash and lots to eat. We have to be full by campfire time, so we aren't tempted to steal somebody's eggs or snack on the bugs who come. It is hard because they look so **delicious,**" said the mother raccoon.

"Tell us about this campfire tonight," asked Max.

"Sorry, no time. Just hang around
by that rock for a little while and you'll
see it all," mother raccoon said, continuing to
dip her food in the clear water.

23

Chapter 4

Fire

Sunset Fire

The sun was beginning to go down, and for the next few minutes Max and Annie were treated to a **western sunset** that painted the wide sky with glorious red, yellow, pink and orange colors. It seemed as if everything in the desert stopped moving as the sun went down and the colors spread across the sky. It was a time of **beauty** and **quiet majesty.** Max and Annie sighed. They had discovered the wondrous glow of the desert. Both dogs bent their heads and took long drinks of the cool water. They knew they should be heading back to their family, but they could not possibly miss the campfire.

Just as they were making the decision to stay a while longer, Max turned his head toward Slippery Rock and saw all kinds of animals forming a large circle. In the middle of the circle was a huge pile of dead trees, scrub brush and logs that was just beginning to smolder.

The campfire was beginning.

Annie and Max ran over and claimed a spot between Chuck, the **lizard,** and a **mule deer doe** and her **fawn.**

Chuck explained to his new friends: "This is our springtime campfire. Twice a year, now and in the late fall, all the animals of the desert gather, prey and predators alike. All agree to put aside their natural desires to eat each other in order to be a part of this magical campfire. There are songs sung, stories told, memories recalled and memories made."

Max and Annie watched excitedly as all the animals arrived. There were **Mexican bats, kangaroo rats, spotted skunks,** and **jack rabbits.** There were **snakes** with **stripes, bands** and blotches, **kit foxes,** and a cute family of **quail.** There were **big horn** and **prong horn sheep** and lots of **raccoons.** They all looked expectantly at Max and Annie.

"Howdy, strangers," said the **desert cottontail.** "It's a tradition that all who are new at the campfire sing a song to start things off. Don't be shy, one of you step up to the mike."

The cottontail handed Max a thick piece of hollowed out wood that looked like a microphone. Never shy and never at a loss for words, Max stood in the middle of the circle and cleared his throat. He whispered to the lizard, and Chuck took out his blues **harmonica** to accompany Max's song.

Ra ra ra ra
OWWWW —howl
Ra ra ra ra
w w w w —whine
Ra ra ra ra
ha ha ha ha —pant
Boom boom boom —drum beat
ra ra ra ra ra ra.

Ra ra ra ra
snap/snap

I'm Maxwell Dog **OWWWW**
of Chagrin Falls. **w w w w**
In the woods I'm the king of it all.

<Max repeats the refrain>

Got lots of friends **OWWWW**
By the score, **w w w w**
and my very own little doggie door.

<Refrain>

In northern Ohio, **OWWWW**
I hunt and run. **w w w w**
I just love bein' out in the sun.

<Refrain>

Some people say **OWWWW**
I'm kinda rude. **w w w w**
They don't know I'm a very cool dude.

<Refrain>

I'm Maxwell Dog **OWWWW**
of Chagrin Falls. **w w w w**
In the woods I'm the king of it all.

Oh, yeh, I'm the...**GRRRR**

Max was just getting warmed up when
he heard a long, loud, low pitched growl. GRRRR . . .

Instantly, everyone was very quiet, and mothers grabbed their children. The growl started again, only this time it ended in a roar. GRRRROAR!! It was the **mountain lion!** He was slowly stalking the group, circling them on the outside of the campfire ring. All the animals were **terrified.**

The lion was a well known bully and was not coming in peace like the rest of the creatures.

While all who knew the mountain lion trembled in fear, Max was just plain mad. He didn't like being interrupted. He had been rolling along, singing his own praises, and he did not want to stop.

"Who does this guy think he is?"

Max demanded loudly.

Chuck whispered, "He's the mountain lion I told you about, and he's the **biggest bully** in the canyon. He could eat us all for breakfast."

"Oh, phooey!" exclaimed Max. "I'm not afraid of him!"

"Well, maybe you should be, Max!" Annie said softly.

"Listen to this," boasted Max. "I'll get rid of him."

All the animals drew in a sharp breath. Bullying a bully was not a good idea. But Max wasn't about to take any advice. He yelled out in his loudest voice.

"Hey you, lion. You interrupted my song. **Apologize, buddy!**"

The mountain lion stopped in his tracks. Everything was eerily silent.

Chapter 5

SHADOWS

The Wall of Shadows

Max yelled out again, **"You call yourself a lion?** Why, I've treed better cats than you in my neighborhood. You call those claws, go get a manicure, **scaredy cat!"**

All the animals gasped, but Max was on a roll. The campfire was burning bright, throwing shadows on the canyon walls that made Max look and feel bigger than he really was. The lion gave a huge roar in response to Max's cat insults. Still, Max wasn't afraid.

The lion was amazed that anyone in this group dared to insult him. This had never happened before! So he stopped his **prowling** and **growling** to listen to the creature in the middle of the circle. The lion couldn't see Max, but he wondered who was brave enough or **crazy** enough to challenge him. He knew, and they all knew, that he could eat every one of them if he wanted to. The big cat roared another time just to keep everyone frightened.

RRRRROAR!

Max ignored the roar and went on with his taunting. "What a coward you are, sneaking around in the dark. You call that a roar? I've heard better from a house cat named Frufru!"

This insult made the big cat **furious.** He started roaring and threatening every creature in the circle. What had started out as a peaceful gathering was quickly becoming **dangerous.** Worst of all, Max's insults were making the situation worse. The big cat was getting **madder** and **madder** as Max went on.

Annie, who had been very quiet up to this point, knew she had to do something. She quickly but softly whispered to the animals in the circle, including Max, who had finally quieted down.

"This cat hasn't seen Max, so he doesn't know that Max is only a dog. If we make Max seem bigger and more powerful than a mere Springer Spaniel, perhaps we can scare the cat away. **Insulting** him **isn't working,** Max," Annie cautioned.

Max realized his mistake and with a sorrowful look, nodded his head in agreement. Seeing the frightened faces of all the campfire animals had brought Max to his senses. Also he had caught a glimpse of the big cat as he stalked the circle. Max realized that he could not fight the cat and win, and he could see that the other animals might get hurt. **"What should I do, Annie?"** Max pleaded.

Annie leaned over and told Max her plan. Suddenly, Max began to howl his best and loudest howl. It was deafening. As he continued to **bark, howl** and **growl,** he began to **run** quickly around the inner circle of the campfire, kicking up lots of **dust** and **sparks.**

From the outside of the circle where the cat was, Max's shadow on the canyon wall was huge. It looked like the shadow was cast by an enormous creature with fire coming from his fur and mouth. It was an **awesome sight!**

When the mountain lion saw the **shadow** of this **flaming, howling, monster,** he stopped in his tracks. "What kind of beast is this?" he asked himself. "It looks and sounds **incredibly fierce.** What if he breathes fire in my direction? I could get singed or catch on fire! **Yikes . . . I'm out of here!"** the lion said to himself as he bolted out of sight.

Cheers erupted from the campfire animals. **Annie's plan** and **Max's performance** saved their lives. Max collapsed on the ground, panting. Chuck thanked Max and Annie saying, "Bullying a bully never makes things better. In the end, our new friends saved the campfire, not by bullying the bully, but by using their heads to come up with a great plan to fool the lion. Let's give them a western cheer." **"Yahoooo,"** cried all the animals together as Max took a sweeping bow. Max's pride swelled as big as his shadow had been. Annie just smiled and lowered her head modestly.

The rest of the campfire was quiet. Animals told stories and sang songs. Max and Annie fell asleep just as Chuck was finishing his story about how he outsmarted a red-tailed hawk.

Chapter 6

Campfire

The Mysterious Campfire

When they felt the warmth of the sun on their fur, Max and Annie **woke up.**
For a minute, they didn't know where they were. Then they remembered the night before
and the campfire. The dogs looked around for the burned up wood and ashes of the evening
fire, but everything looked as it had before the events of last night. There was no evidence of
a **campfire,** a gathering of **animals, nothing . . .** Max and Annie
were puzzled. Where were the ashes from the fire? Where were the animal tracks?

Just then, Max heard a familiar voice anxiously calling his name. **Maxxx!!** It was Mom, and she sounded pretty angry. He and Annie glanced at each other. They had been out all night, and they knew they were in **big trouble.**

Max and Annie spent the rest of their time in Arizona at the end of their leashes. Max was a little **relieved.** His experience with the mountain lion had humbled him a bit. Just before boarding the plane for Ohio, Max told Annie, "When we were at the campfire, I learned an important lesson about dealing with bullies."

"What was that?" Annie asked with a slight smile on her face.

"I found out that insults and taunting never work; they just make a bad situation worse. I realize now that you have to control your own temper, be sensitive to the feelings of others and use your **head** and your **heart** to work things out," Max said proudly.

Annie nodded knowingly as they both headed for the plane. When they were in their travel crate, munching on some **snacks** Mom got them from first class, Max laughed and said, "I had **fun** here in Arizona, but I'll be **happy** to get home. They have much smaller cats in Ohio!"

Let's Write

List all the things you learned about the desert from the story and the pictures.
(Try to find at least 10 facts!)

How and why did Max get caught up in name calling and bullying?

When did the campfire become dangerous?

What did Max and Annie do to make the campfire safe again?

What did Max and all the animals learn about bullies like the mountain lion?

Have you ever been bullied in school or on the playground?
What did you do? How did it work out?

What would you do if someone was bullying you now that
you have read about Max's experience?

Just for Fun

Try retelling this story from the mountain lion's point of view.

(Use these questions to help you. Was the mountain lion invited to the campfire? Did he feel left out? Did Max start the bullying? Did the mountain lion try to get everyone's attention by bullying Max? Is there another possible happy ending with the mountain lion becoming the hero?)

The Real Max and Annie

Max is now five years old. These days he spends a lot of time visiting children in schools with Annie and his mom, Sandy Philipson. In the last three years, Max and Annie have been to more than 80 schools, and Max has had lots of adventures. In one school, he jumped into a fish tank; in another's cafeteria, he rolled around in mayonnaise and ate three packages of peanut butter crackers before he was caught. One night at a school parents' program, he escaped out the door, chased a cat up a tree, covered himself in burrs, upset some neighborhood garbage cans and chased a bunch of squirrels. He has had so much fun visiting schools that his mom may write another book just about his school misadventures!

Annie, the three-legged Springer, is now twelve years old. (She lost her left front leg to cancer three years ago.) This year she celebrated her birthday on the set of **Miracle Dogs**, a movie produced by TAG Family Entertainment, that stars Max and Annie (and human actors, too). Both Max and Annie took "acting lessons" with a professional dog trainer and their mom and dad. They learned to sit, stay, track, and look sad, thoughtful or happy for the camera. Everyone said they did a great job, especially for beginners.

Miracle Dogs, based on Annie's book, is a story of friendship, inspiration and healing. It emphasizes the sometimes magical relationship between animals and people.

Max and **Annie** have traveled a lot recently, but their favorite places to visit besides schools, are hospitals and/or events for children and families touched by cancer. Both dogs hope that they bring some comfort to children with their soft cuddly ways and their doggie kisses.

Both Max and Annie have special heart markings. Annie has hers on her head, and Max has a large heart on his side. See if you can spot the hearts in their pictures.

Other books in the Max and Annie series are: <u>Annie Loses Her Leg But Finds Her Way</u>, <u>Max's Wild Goose Chase</u>, and <u>The Artist: A Max and Annie Adventure in Imagination.</u>

You can visit Max and Annie on their web site at **www.maxandannie.com**.

53

Max's Campfire Song

Music by Janie Reinart

Words by Sandy Philipson and Janie Reinart
Arranged by Mark Coming

(REFRAIN)Ra ra ra ra(owwwww) Ra ra ra

ra(mmmmm) Ra ra ra ra(huhuhuh) Boom boom boom ra ra ra ra ra

ra. 1.Ra ra ra ra(snap/snap) I'm Max-well Dog(owwwww) of Chag- rin

Falls(mmmmm) In the woods I'm the king of it all.

Music Consultant: Christie Dilisio
© 2002 Janie Reinart

\<Refrain\>
Ra ra ra ra
OWWWW —howl
Ra ra ra ra
ʍ ʍ ʍ ʍ —whine
Ra ra ra ra
ha ha ha ha —pant
Boom boom boom —**drum beat**
ra ra ra ra ra ra.

Ra ra ra ra
snap/snap

1. I'm Maxwell Dog **OWWWW**
of Chagrin Falls. **ʍ ʍ ʍ ʍ**
In the woods I'm the king of it all.

\<Refrain\>

2. Got lots of friends **OWWWW**
By the score, **ʍ ʍ ʍ ʍ**
and my very own little doggie door.

\<Refrain\>

3. In northern Ohio, **OWWWW**
I hunt and run. **ʍ ʍ ʍ ʍ**
I just love bein' out in the sun.

\<Refrain\>

4. Some people say **OWWWW**
I'm kinda rude. **ʍ ʍ ʍ ʍ**
They don't know I'm a very cool dude.

\<Refrain\>

5. I'm Maxwell Dog **OWWWW**
of Chagrin Falls. **ʍ ʍ ʍ ʍ**
In the woods I'm the king of it all.

Oh, yeh, I'm the ...GRRRR

Pawtographs

Max

Annie